Walt Disney's Lady

From the motion picture "Lady and The Tramp"
Based on the story by Ward Greene

Pictures by the WALT DISNEY STUDIO

Adapted by ALLAN HUBBARD and GENE WOLFE

A WHITMAN BOOK
Western Publishing Company, Inc.
Racine, Wisconsin

Copyright © MCMLIV by Walt Disney Productions
World rights reserved. Produced in the U.S.A.

WHITMAN and TELL-A-TALE are registered trademarks of Western Publishing Company, Inc. No part of this book may be reproduced or copied in any form without written permission from the publisher.

Lady was a beautiful spaniel with long silky ears and a ladylike bark. Jim Dear and Darling loved her and gave her everything a little dog could possibly want.

She had her own dishes with LADY printed neatly in blue, in a wreath of pink flowers.

Lady had a bed of her own but she preferred to sleep at the foot of Jim Dear's or Darling's bed, where she was always welcome.

There were trips to the Pet Shop where Lady's fur and nails were trimmed. She liked to look in the big mirror and she always came away with a new ribbon bow.

When it rained Lady wore a little red raincoat which was the envy of the neighborhood dogs.

"She's lovely!" said Jock.

"She's the only dog I know who has a raincoat," said Trusty.

Lady had smooth bones to chew—delicious after they had been buried in the garden. But Lady never once disturbed the flower beds. That was the way she showed her family that she loved them.

"I wish I could do more for them," said Lady, one day, to her friends Jock and Trusty. "But what can a little dog do?"

"You could carry things for them," suggested Trusty.

"And bring things to them," said Jock, trying to be helpful.

So—Lady learned to carry a package of meat without tearing the paper.

And she learned to catch the newspaper when the boy tossed it.

When she took the paper to Jim Dear he always patted her and said, "Good Lady! Good dog!"

Lady was the happiest little dog in the whole world until the day—

—a baby came to live with Jim Dear and Darling. Then—Lady was sent to her kennel to sleep.

Everyone was excited and busy and no one paid any attention to poor lonesome Lady.

"They don't love me any more," said Lady when she told Trusty and Jock about the baby.

"Having family trouble?" It was a new voice—a rough voice. Lady looked at the strange dog.

"Families are no good," said the dog. "I haven't a regular family and I get along fine."

The dog gave a gay whistle and off he trotted, his ears and tail waving in the breeze.

"Who is he?" asked Lady.

"His name's Tramp," said Jock.

"He's rough and a bit braggy," added Trusty. "But Tramp's really not a bad fellow."

When Lady joined her friends the next day, Tramp was with them.

"Why the tears?" he asked.

"Today's Saturday," sobbed Lady, "and they're so busy with the baby they've forgotten my bath."

"Baths aren't important," said Tramp. "Why don't you run away with me? We'll have fun and your family won't miss you."

Just then Jock and Trusty were called in to dinner. No one called Lady. She felt very lonely. So—when Tramp whistled and ran after a wagon, Lady followed without as much as a glance at her home.

Lady never forgot that evening.
What a wonderful time they had!
They chased a cat up a tree.

They jumped over fences.

They barked at the moon.

But by and by Lady's soft little feet began to hurt. So when Tramp chased a rat down an alley, Lady sat near a basement window and waited for him.

Lady loved to look in mirrors and shiny windows. While she waited for Tramp to come back, she glanced at her reflection in the window.

What she saw made her jump in fright. She looked around. She expected to see a strange dog. But no other dog was there. She looked in the window again. Lady couldn't believe her eyes. She stared and stared. Then she hid her face in her paws.

"Oh!" she cried. "I'm not a lady. I'm just an ugly little dog with muddy fur and a dirty, torn ribbon. I *hate* looking like this."

"You missed some fun," Tramp said later as he sat beside her. "That rat—why, Lady! You're crying. What's the matter?"

"I want to go home," sobbed Lady. "Take me home, Tramp, please."

"Well," said Tramp gently, "I'll take you home if you want me to. But I think it's a mistake."

Tramp knew a short cut and soon they were walking up the steps of Lady's home. Jim Dear was at the door. Beyond him Lady saw dinner waiting for her—and there on a chair were her bath things.

"Lady!" cried Jim Dear. "What do you mean by running away? Don't you know we're going to need a dog to look after the baby?"

Lady gave a soft grateful bark.

Then Tramp wagged his tail and barked *very politely*.

"Well," said Jim Dear. "Bring your friend in, Lady. I think we can use two dogs around here to help with the baby."

Lady was happy to know that Jim Dear and Darling wanted her. And Tramp was happy to have a home with Lady. He didn't even mind bath days *too* much. But the baby was happiest of all because he had *two* dogs to play with and take care of him.